BEETHOVEN
PIANO SONATA NO. 8
Op. 13
PATHETIQUE

EDITED BY ARTUR SCHNABEL

WITH TEXT IN:
ENGLISH, SPANISH,, ITALIAN,
GERMAN, FRENCH

SONATA N. 8 (Patetica)

(Dedicata al Principe Carlo von Lichnowsky)

Composta nell'anno 1798
Pubblicata nel 1799
presso Eder, a Vienna

Op. 13

a) Corona della durata di 7 trentaduesimi circa.

a) *About 7 demisemiquavers long.*

a) Etwa sieben Zweiunddreissigstel lang.

a) *Point d'orgue d'une durée d'environ triples-croches.*

a) Calderón de más o menos 7 fusas de duración.

4

a)

oppure:
or:
oder:

b) Come nell' Edizione Urtext. La maggior parte delle edizioni hanno:

b) *According to the «Urtext» edition. Most editions have:*

b) Nach der Urtextausgabe. Die meisten Ausgaben haben:

Non vi è ragione di aggiungere il *do*, basandosi sul passaggio corrispondente, che però modula in modo diverso.

The parallel passage which modulates differently can not be used as reason for adding the «c» here.

Die Parallelstelle, die modulatorisch anders verläuft, kann zur Begründung des zugefügten c² nicht herangezogen werden.

For French and Spanish notes see page 24

attacca subito l'Allegro molto e con brio

a) Alcune edizioni hanno il *p* già sul primo quarto.

b) Corona della durata di 5 minime circa. Senza pausa.

c) Corona della durata di 7 minime circa. Segue una pausa del valore di due minime (naturalmente senza pedale).

d) Corona della durata di 5 ottavi circa. Senza pausa.

a) *Some editions have « p » already on the first crotchet.*

b) *Fermata about 5 minims; no pause afterwards.*

c) *Fermata about 7 minims, then 2 minims pause (naturally without pedal).*

d) *Fermata about 5 quavers long; no pause afterwards.*

a) Manche haben *p* schon zum ersten Viertel.

b) Fermate etwa 5 Halbe; keine Luftpause danach.

c) Fermate etwa 7 Halbe; danach 2 Halbe Luftpause (selbstverständlich ohne Pedal).

d) Fermate etwa 5 Achtel lang: keine Luftpause danach.

For French and Spanish notes see page 24

Allegro molto e con brio

a) Vedi pag. 4 a).   a) *See page 4 a).* a).   a) Siehe Seite 4 a).

a) *Voir page 4 a)*   a) Mirar pag. 4 a)

a) Corona della durata di 7 minime circa. Poi alzare il pedale.
b) Attenzione alla corona.

a) *Fermata about 7 minims; then release the pedal.*
b) *Observe the Fermata!*

a) Fermate etwa 7 Halbe; danach Pedal aufheben.
b) Fermate beachten!

a) *Point d'orgue d'environ la valeur de sept blanches; lever ensuite la pédale.*
b) *Tenir compte du point d'orgue.*

a) Calderón de la duración aproximada de 7 blancas; luego quitar el pedal.
b) Tener en cuenta el calderón.

a)

b) All'accordo sulla quarta croma a volte manca il *re*.

c) Alcune edizioni omettono la forcella del crescendo.

b) *In some editions the «d» in the chord on the fourth quaver is missing.*

c) *Some editions omit the crescendo symbol.*

b) Bei Manchen fehlt das *d* im Akkord des vierten Achtels.

c) Die Gabel fehlt bei Einigen.

b) *A l'accord au quatrième temps, il manque parfois le ré.*

c) *Certains reviseurs omettent le soufflet.*

b) En el acorde en el cuarto tiempo, talvez falta el *re*.

c) Algunos revisores omiten la horquilla del crescendo.

a) L'Edizione Critica Completa ha tanto qui quanto alla battuta seguente il segno *rf* sul primo tempo della battuta. Questo segno manca nella Edizione Urtext.

a) The « Kritische Gesamtausgabe » has « rf » on the first beat of this as well as the following bar. In the « Urtext » edition there is no such indication.

a) Die Kritische Gesamtausgabe hat hier, und ebenso im folgenden Takt, auf dem ersten Achtel das Zeichen *rf*. In der Urtextausgabe steht es hingegen nicht.

a) Ici, de même qu'à la mesure suivante, l'Edition Critique Générale place le signe «*rf*» a la première croche de la mesure. Ce «*rf*» fait défaut dans l'édition originale.

a) Aquí, lo mismo que en el compás siguiente, la Edición Critica General marca *rf* a la primera corchea del compás Este *rf* falta en la edición original.

a)

b) Attenzione alla corona! | b) *Observe the Fermata!* | b) Fermate beachten!
b) *Tenir compte du point d'orgue.* | b) Tener en cuenta el calderón.

RONDÒ

Allegro (♩ = 100 - 108)

a) Alcune edizioni hanno il segno *sf* sul terzo quarto. Altre, invece, non l'hanno affatto.

b) Corona della durata di 4 minime circa. Senza pausa.

a) Some editions have the sign «sf» on the third beat, others again omit it entirely.

b) Fermata about 4 minims. No pause afterwards.

a) Manche haben das Zeichen *sf* zum dritten Viertel, andere wiederum haben es überhaupt nicht.

b) Fermate etwa 4 Halbe; keine Luftpause danach.

(v. p.202b)

a) In alcune edizioni la quinta (e la nona) croma delle terzine sono *fa*.

a) *In some editions the fifth (and ninth) triplet quaver is «f».*

a) Bei Einigen heisst das fünfte (und neunte) Triolenachtel *f*.

a) *Dans certaines éditions, la cinquième (et neuvième) valeur des triolets doivent être* fa.

a) En algunas ediciones la quinta (y la nona) corchea de los tresillos es un *fa*.

a) Corona della durata di 5 minime circa. Senza pausa.
b) Attenzione alla corona!

a) *Fermata about 5 minims. No pause afterwards.*
b) *Observe the Fermata!*

a) Fermate etwa 5 Halbe. Keine Luftpause danach.
b) Fermate beachten!

a) *Point d'orgue d'une durée de la valeur d'environ cinq blanches; ne faire suivre d'aucune pause.*
b) *Tenir compte du point d'orgue.*

a) Calderón de la duración aproximadamente de cinco blancas, sin hacer seguir de ninguna pausa.
b) Tener en cuenta el calderón.

Continued from page 4

b) *Conforme à l'édition originale. La plupart des éditions ont:*

Le passage correspondant, d'uneautre modulation, ne peut servir de comparaison justificative pour l'adjonction du do *à la octave.*

b) Conforme a la edición original. La mayor parte de las ediciones tienen:

El paso correspondiente, de otra modulación, ne puede servir de comparación justificante por la añadidura del *do.*

Continued from page 6

a) *Certains reviseurs placent le «p» déjà au premier temps.*

b) *Point d'orgue d'une durée d'environ la valeur de cinq blanches; ne faire suivre d'aucune pause.*

c) *Point d'orgue d'une durée d'environ la valeur de sept blanches; faire suivre d'un arret correspondant à la valeur de deux blanches (évidemment sans pédale).*

d) *Point d'orgue d'une durée d'environ la valeur de cinq croches; ne faire suivre d'aucune pause.*

a) Algunas ediciones ponen *p* desde el primer cuarto.

b) Calderón de la duración aproximadamente del valor de cinco blancas, sin hacer seguir otra pausa.

c) Calderón de la duración aproximadamente del valor de 7 blancas, hacer seguir un silencio correspondiente al valor de 2 blancas (evidentemente sin pedal).

d) Calderón de la duración aproximada de 5 corcheas sin hacer seguir ninguna pausa.

Continued from page 18

a) *Certaines editions ont le signe: sf au troisieme temps; d'autres editions, par contre, ne le donnentpas du tout.*

b) *Point d'orgue d'une duree de la valeur d'environ quatre blanches. Ne faire suivre d'aucune pause.*

a) Algunas ediciones tienen el signo *sf* al tercer tiempo, en otras ediciones al reves no lo ponen.

b) Calderon de la duracion de 4 blancas. Sin pausa.